AN ARK FULL
OF
ACTIVITIES

CLAIRE FREEDMAN

Marshall Pickering
An Imprint of HarperCollinsPublishers

TO MY FATHER, WITH LOVE

Marshall Pickering is an Imprint of
HarperCollins*Religious*
Part of HarperCollins*Publishers*
77–85 Fulham Palace Road, London W6 8JB
www.christian-publishing.com

First published in Great Britain in 2000
by Marshall Pickering

1 3 5 7 9 10 8 6 4 2

Copyright © 2000 Claire Freedman

Claire Freedman asserts the moral right to be identified
as the author of this work

A catalogue record for this book is available from the British Library

ISBN 0 551 03242 1

Printed and bound in Great Britain by
Martins the Printers, Berwick upon Tweed

CONTENTS

HANDY HINTS   5

1.   WONDERFUL CREATION!   6
     Sun, Moon and Stars Mobile   7

2.   IN GOD'S GARDEN   10
     Trees in the Garden   11

3.   SNAKE IN THE GRASS!   13
     Sneaky Snake Pot   14

4.   ALL IN THE ARK   16
     Noah's Animal Skittles   17

5.   REBEKAH AT THE WELL   19
     Glittering Gold Necklace   20

6.   JOSEPH THE DREAMER   22
     Technicolour T-Shirts   23

7.   WANDERING IN THE DESERT   26
     Desert Scene Theatre   27

8.   MOSES RECEIVES THE LAW FROM GOD   32
     Scrolls   33

9.   SPIES ON A MISSION   35
     Secret Codes and Messages   36

10. BALAAM'S TALKING DONKEY   38
     Dinky Donkey   39

11. SAVED BY A SCARLET CORD   43
     Colourful Cords! Beautiful Braids!   44

12. SAMSON THE SUPER-STRONG   46
     Hairy Samson   47

13. **DAVID THE SHEPHERD BOY**   **50**
    Snazzy Sheep Coat Hooks   51

14. **THE QUEEN OF SHEBA BRINGS GIFTS TO SOLOMON**   **54**
    Great Gift Boxes   55

15. **DANIEL AND THE DANGEROUS LIONS**   **57**
    Lion Photograph Frame   58

16. **JONAH AND THE GREAT WHALE**   **61**
    Big Fish Money Box   62

HANDY HINTS

Before you begin making anything, always remember these important rules:

1   Always ask an adult for help when you need to use a craft knife.

2   Always handle scissors with the points facing away from you.

3   Put pins and needles away after you have finished using them.

4   Always wear oven gloves when putting things into or taking them out of the oven (e.g. salt dough pieces).

5   Always ask an adult for help when you use the iron. Remember to switch the iron off after you have finished using it.

6   Use varnish and glues carefully, and only in a well ventilated room.

7   Before you start to make anything, read the instructions through and make sure you have everything you need.

8   If you are using anything messy, put on an apron and cover your work surface with newspaper.

9   When you have finished, always remember to clean and tidy everything up.

1. WONDERFUL CREATION!

In the beginning God created the heavens and the earth. At first the earth was a swirling mass, empty, unformed and in total darkness. Then God said, 'Let there be light!' and light appeared, separating day from night.

God made the land and the seas. He clothed the dry land with grass and plants, and trees of every kind. He made the sun and the moon, and stars to shine in the sky.

Then he said, 'Let the oceans swarm with fish, and the air be filled with birds. Let animals live on the land.' So the earth became a home to countless wonderful living creatures.

Lastly, God made man and woman, in his own likeness. 'Take charge of my world,' God told them. 'I give everything to you.'

God's work took him six days, and on the seventh day he rested. But one day is like a thousand years to God, and a thousand years like one day.

Genesis 1–2

Sun, Moon and Stars Mobile

YOU WILL NEED:

stiff white card

paper (for templates)

a pencil

scissors

a needle

strong thread

gold, silver, yellow and orange paints and brushes

PVA glue and brush

1 Cut out a circle of card about 10cm (4in) in diameter. Paint it gold on both sides. Leave to dry.

2 Using a needle, punch a ring of 6 holes around the card rim. Each hole should be about 1cm (½in) from the outside edge, and spaced evenly.

3 Draw sun, moon and star shapes onto paper. Cut out the shapes. Place these paper templates on top of the remaining card. Draw around each one and cut out the shapes. You will need 8 stars, 4 suns and 4 moons to make the mobile shown in the picture.

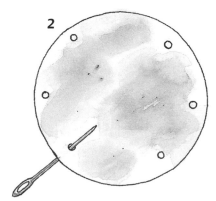

stiff   card

4

4 Paint the stars gold and the moons silver, on one side only. Paint 2 of the sun shapes bright orange and the other 2 yellow. Paint the suns on both sides. Leave to dry.

5 Cut 6 lengths of thread, each about 45cm (18in) long.

6 Thread the needle with one length of thread. Push the needle up through one of the holes on the card circle. Then bring the needle back up through the same hole again. Gently pull the thread up to tighten it. Repeat with the other lengths of thread on the remaining 5 holes.

7 Hold the 6 lengths of thread together at the top. Gently pull them up to an equal length of approximately 20cm (8in) above the card circle. Tie the ends together with a firm knot.

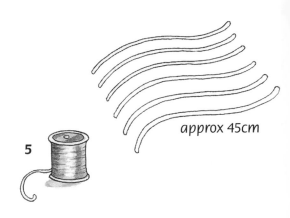

approx 45cm

5

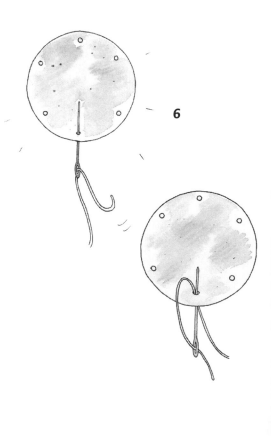

6

7

← 20cm

← 25cm

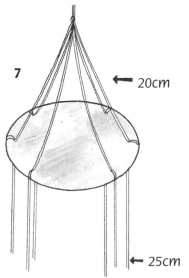

8

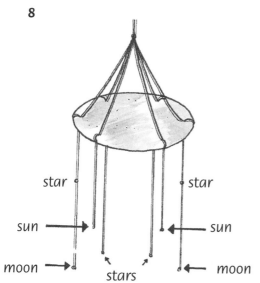

star   star

sun ⟶   ⟵ sun

moon ⟶   ⟵ moon

stars

8   Decide where you want to position the stars, suns and moons on the mobile. To help the mobile hang properly, each shape must be balanced evenly.

9   Paste glue on the wrong side of one of the stars. Lay the thread over the sticky side in the position you want. Place another star on top, with the painted side upwards, sliding it into place so that all the points match. Press together firmly.

9

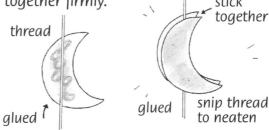

thread

glued

stick together

glued   snip thread to neaten

10 Attach the suns to the thread in the same way, using one orange and one yellow half for each sun. Only put glue in the middle of the sun shape. Swivel the 2 suns to make a multicoloured 'sunburst' effect.

10

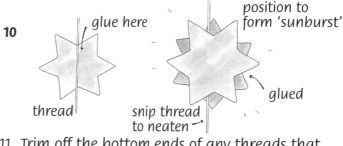

glue here

thread

snip thread to neaten

position to form 'sunburst'

glued

11 Trim off the bottom ends of any threads that show. Leave to dry. Your mobile is now ready to hang up.

11

Tips and Ideas

☀ Try sticking glitter or sequins to your mobile, or use gold and silver card instead of paint.

☀ You could make a cloud, sun and rainbow mobile.

2. IN GOD'S GARDEN

God planted a beautiful garden in the east, in Eden. There he placed the first man he made, called Adam.

In the middle of the garden grew two trees – the Tree of Life and the Tree of the Knowledge of Good and Evil.

'You may freely eat the fruit of any tree or plant,' God told Adam, 'but on the day you eat the fruit from the Tree of the Knowledge of Good and Evil you will surely die.'

God brought all the animals and birds to Adam, and Adam gave each and every one of them a name. But God soon saw that none of the creatures he had made were a suitable companion for Adam.

'It isn't good for man to live alone,' God said. 'I will make a partner fit for him.'

So God sent Adam into a deep, deep sleep. While Adam slept, God opened up his side and took out one of his ribs. From this rib he made a woman, called Eve.

Eve became Adam's wife, and together they spent their days happily tending God's garden.

Genesis 2

Trees in the Garden

YOU WILL NEED:

a 7.5cm (3in) plastic plant pot

Plasticine

a dry twig or stick from the garden, about 19cm (7½in) long (choose a strong, straight stick and pull off any leaves)

a small plastic foam sphere (available from florist shops)

small, clean pebbles from the garden or beach

dried flowers, grasses and seed heads

a small piece of narrow ribbon

scissors

1   Place a large blob of Plasticine in the bottom of the plant pot. Push the stick into the centre.

2   Take the foam sphere and place it on top of the stick, pushing the end of the stick about 5cm (2in) into the sphere.

3   Fill the pot with pebbles, placing them carefully around the stick, until they reach the rim of the pot. Make sure the stick stays upright.

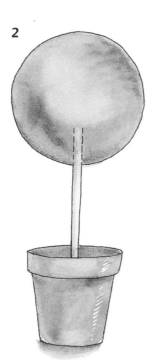

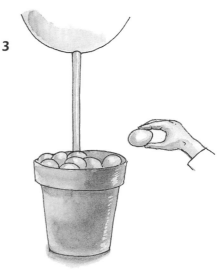

4   Push the dried flowers into the foam sphere. Keep the stems short – no longer than 2–3cm (1in) – and push the flowers in up to their heads. If you are using dried grasses, break off small shoots. Carry on sticking in flowers all around the sphere until it is completely covered and no plastic foam can be seen.

5   Tie the ribbon in a pretty bow around the bottom of the stick. Remember to keep your tree away from direct sunlight, to stop the flowers from fading.

Tips and Ideas

☀   The best dried flowers to buy include strawflowers (Helichrysum), hydrangea florets, chrysanthemums, small rosebuds, statice (or sea lavender) and all daisy-type flowers. Look out for attractive seed heads and grasses too.

☀   It is easy to make your own dried flowers and grasses. Simply tie the flowers in small bunches and hang them up in a dry, airy room. Some flowers will take a few weeks to dry. Always ask permission before you pick anything from the garden.

☀   You can also make this tree using artificial flowers.

☀   Instead of pebbles, try decorating the top of your pot with pretty shells.

3. SNAKE IN THE GRASS!

The serpent lived in the garden of Eden. It was the most cunning creature God had made. One day it sidled up to Eve and whispered, 'Did God say you could eat the fruit of any tree?'

'Yes,' Eve replied. 'Except the fruit of the Tree of the Knowledge of Good and Evil, of course. If we eat that – we die!'

'You won't die,' the snake answered. 'God knows that if you eat the fruit you will become wise like him.'

Eve longed to be wise and was tempted to try the fruit. She also gave some to Adam.

But straight away everything changed. Adam and Eve realized they were naked and felt ashamed. Quickly they sewed fig leaves together to cover themselves, and hid from God. But God saw them and was angry.

'You have done the one thing I forbade you to do,' God said. 'You can no longer stay here. Now you will have to go out into the world to make a living.'

God also punished the serpent. Adam and Eve sadly left the garden, never to return.

Genesis 3

Sneaky Snake Pot

This snake coil pot makes a great pen and pencil holder. It is made from salt dough, which you can make yourself easily and cheaply.

YOU WILL NEED:

300g (12oz) plain flour

100g (4oz) salt

2 teaspoons of oil

225–350ml (7–12fl oz) warm water

plastic bag

greaseproof paper

baking tray

poster paints and brushes

clear varnish

1 Mix the flour, salt and oil together in a bowl. Stir in the water, a little at a time, until you have a ball of soft but not sticky dough.

2 Knead the dough on a floured surface until it is smooth and elastic. Then place it in a plastic bag and leave in the fridge for 1 hour before using.

3 Pull off a piece of dough the size of a ping pong ball. Roll it into a ball, then flatten it with your hands to make a circle about 6cm (2½in) wide and 5mm (¼in) thick. This will be the base of the pot. Sprinkle some flour onto a sheet of greaseproof paper. Place the circle of dough onto the paper.

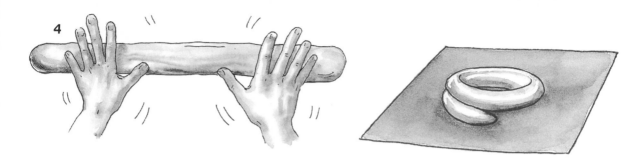

4

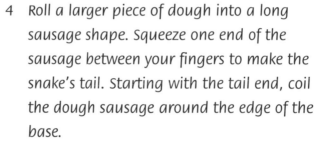

5

6

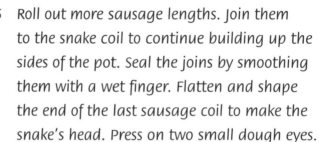

4   Roll a larger piece of dough into a long sausage shape. Squeeze one end of the sausage between your fingers to make the snake's tail. Starting with the tail end, coil the dough sausage around the edge of the base.

5   Roll out more sausage lengths. Join them to the snake coil to continue building up the sides of the pot. Seal the joins by smoothing them with a wet finger. Flatten and shape the end of the last sausage coil to make the snake's head. Press on two small dough eyes.

6   Place the pot with the paper onto a baking tray. Bake in a preheated oven at gas mark 3/170°C/325°F, until the pot is hard. This should take about 1$\frac{1}{2}$–2$\frac{1}{2}$ hours.

7   Remove the pot from the oven, wearing oven gloves. When it has cooled, peel off the baking paper. Paint the snake and leave it to dry. Finally, finish off with a coat of varnish and let it dry.

7

4. ALL IN THE ARK

As people grew more and more wicked, God was sorry that he had ever created humankind. So he decided to wash the world clean with a flood.

But one man, Noah, was good and deserved to be spared. God told Noah to build a huge boat. 'Take aboard your wife and family,' God said, 'also a male and female of every kind of animal and bird, together with plenty of food.'

Noah got to work and then, as God foretold, the rains came. It rained for 40 days and 40 nights, and every living creature on earth was drowned. Only those in the ark were alive, floating safely above the water.

When at last the waters dropped, the ark came to rest on Mount Ararat. Noah sent out a raven and a dove, to see if they could find dry land. But each time the birds flew back, finding nowhere to perch. Once more he released the dove, and when it did not return, Noah knew it was safe to leave the ark.

God told Noah, 'Never again will I destroy the world with a flood. The rainbow in the sky is the sign of my promise.'

Genesis 6–8

Noah's Animal Skittles

YOU WILL NEED:

newspaper

cardboard tubes (one for each skittle)

sticky tape

scraps of thick card

a pencil

scissors

PVA glue (diluted 2 parts glue to 1 part water) or flour paste, and brush (to make your own flour paste see the recipe below)

paints and brushes

clear varnish

TO MAKE FLOUR PASTE

YOU WILL NEED:

1 cup of flour

3 cups of water

a large saucepan

a wooden spoon
This quantity makes about 1¹/₂cups of paste. Ask an adult for help when using the stove.

1 Put the flour in the saucepan. Gradually stir in 1 cup of water. Mix well with the wooden spoon into a smooth paste.

2 Add the other 2 cups of water. Mix well to get rid of any lumps.

3 Heat the mixture until it boils, stirring all the time. As soon as it has thickened, turn off the heat. Allow to cool before using.

TO MAKE THE SKITTLES

1 Tightly scrunch up some newspaper into your chosen animal head shape – a tight ball if you are making a monkey or lion, a more elongated head shape for a giraffe or zebra, etc. Tape the head to one end of a cardboard tube.

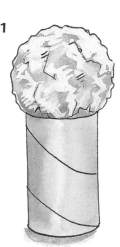

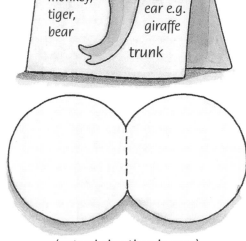

(actual size tiger's ears)

2 Fold a piece of card in half. Draw 2 ear shapes, making sure the tip of each ear is positioned at the fold. Cut around the ear shape, but do not cut through the fold. (Make an elephant's trunk in the same way, by positioning the tip of the trunk at the fold.)

3 Slightly open out the ears (or trunk), and tape into position on the head.

4 Tear some newspaper into small strips. Brush each strip with glue or paste and use to cover the head completely. Build up 3 layers of newspaper to give a smooth finish. Cover the tube with one layer of paper. Leave the papier-maché to dry thoroughly (this may take about a day).

5 Paint the skittle all over with white paint. Allow to dry.

6 Now paint the skittle brightly in its animal colours. Leave to dry.

7 Finally, brush on 2 layers of clear varnish to give the skittles a shiny finish and to stop them from chipping. Use a soft sponge ball when playing with your skittles.

3

4

5

6 & 7

-18-

5. REBEKAH AT THE WELL

Abraham had a great faith in God. He left his home in Haran to live in Canaan, the land God had promised to give him and his descendants for ever.

When Abraham was very old he called his loyal servant. 'I do not want my son Isaac to marry a Canaanite woman,' Abraham said. 'Go back to my homeland and find a wife for him there.'

The servant set off with 10 camels and many gifts. He arrived at the well outside the city as evening fell – the time the women came to draw water from the well.

'Oh Lord,' he prayed, 'let the girl whom I ask for a drink from the well be the right wife for Isaac.'

Before he had even finished praying, a beautiful young girl called Rebekah arrived. She gladly gave the servant a drink and drew water for his camels too.

The servant was overjoyed to discover that Rebekah was related to Abraham, and gave her presents of gold jewellery.

Rebekah invited him to meet her family, and everyone agreed it was clearly God's will for her to marry Isaac. The very next day she left her home and travelled with the servant back to Canaan. When Isaac and Rebekah met, they fell in love immediately – and very soon they were married.

Genesis 24

Glittering Gold Necklace

In Bible times, men often gave their brides gold jewellery to wear – it showed everyone how wealthy they were!

YOU WILL NEED:

salt dough (see recipe and Steps 1 and 2 for the Sneaky Snake Pot, page 14)

straight-sided kebab skewers

baking tray

gold and silver paints and brushes

clear varnish

thin gold cord

scissors

a needle

1 Pull off small pieces of dough. Make round beads by rolling the dough into balls. For longer, flatter beads roll out thin sausage shapes then flatten the edges slightly with your fingers. For this necklace you will need to make 12 round beads and 5 flatter beads.

2

flatten at sides

Push the beads onto the skewers, making the holes in the long beads a little way in from one end. Balance the skewers across a baking tray so that the beads are suspended. Bake in a preheated oven at gas mark 2/150°C/300°F for about $^{1}/_{2}$–$1^{1}/_{2}$ hours, until the beads are hard.

2

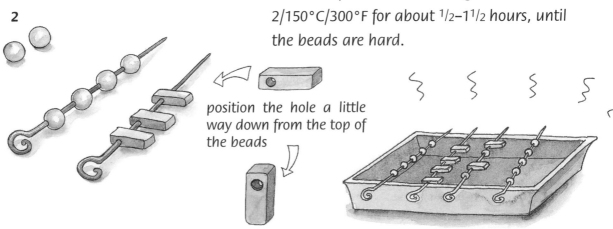

position the hole a little way down from the top of the beads

3 When the beads have cooled, paint the round beads gold and the flatter beads silver. Leave to dry, then varnish.

4 When the varnish is dry, cut a length of gold cord a little longer than you want your necklace to be. Make sure it is big enough to go over your head. Thread a needle with the cord and push on 4 round beads, then a flatter bead, followed by a round bead and so on, as shown in the picture, finishing with 4 round beads. Knot the ends of the cord tightly.

Tips and Ideas

☼ To make a bracelet, thread beads onto fine elastic.

☼ To colour and varnish your beads in one go, paint them with brightly coloured nail varnish – glitter nail varnish looks really good!

☼ Try adding colour to your dough by kneading in drops of food colouring. If the dough becomes sticky, knead in more flour.

6. JOSEPH THE DREAMER

Joseph lived in Canaan with his father Jacob, his mother and 11 brothers.

Joseph was his father's favourite. When he was 17, Jacob gave him a beautiful new coat which filled his elder brothers with envy. This was no ordinary coat – it was long with full sleeves, woven in many brilliant colours.

'I had a dream last night,' Joseph told his brothers. 'We were all in a field tying up sheaves of corn. My sheaf stood up and your sheaves gathered round and bowed down to it!'

His brothers were furious. 'So – you think you'll rule over us!' they cried angrily.

Joseph had another dream. 'I dreamt that the sun, moon and 11 stars all bowed down to me!' he said.

Even his father grew cross over that dream. 'Must we all bow before you – as if you were a king?' he said.

One day the brothers were on the plains minding their father's sheep. They saw Joseph coming towards them in the distance. How they hated him!

'Here comes the dreamer,' they mocked. And they plotted to kill him.

Genesis 37

Technicolour T-shirts

Before you start, read the instructions on the fabric paints. It is a good idea to practise on a spare piece of fabric, before you begin painting your T-shirt. If you are using a new T-shirt, wash it first to remove any dressing in the fabric.

YOU WILL NEED:

a white cotton T-shirt (washed and ironed)

masking tape

pieces of thick cardboard

scissors

fabric paints in crimson red, yellow and blue

a small sponge pan cleaner

3 saucers

1   First find the middle of the T-shirt by folding it in half, matching the sleeves. Mark the middle with masking tape at the top and bottom of the fold. Open the T-shirt out and decide where you want to position the centre of your design. Fold the T-shirt from top to bottom at this point, and mark the fold on each side with masking tape. Use the masking tape as a guide to help keep your design even as you work.

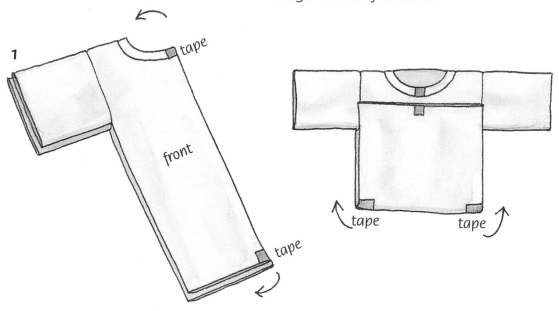

1

tape

front

tape

tape

tape

2 To stop fabric paint from soaking through to
   the back of the T-shirt, cut pieces of card
   and insert them into the body and sleeves of
   the T-shirt. The card should fit snugly in
   position, without stretching the fabric.

3 Pour a little of the different coloured fabric
   paints into 3 separate saucers. Cut off three
   small wedges from the sponge.

4 Lightly dip a corner of one of the sponge
   pieces into the red fabric paint. Following
   your masking tape guidelines, sponge on a
   splodge of colour in the centre of the T-shirt.

2

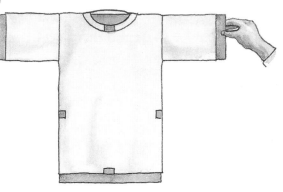

3

5 Using a clean piece of sponge and the
   yellow paint, sponge on dabs of yellow paint
   all around the red splodge. Let the paint
   colours overlap a little to give a rainbow
   effect. Using the third clean sponge piece,
   dab blue fabric paint around the yellow
   circle, letting the colours merge as before.
   Repeat using the red colour again, and so
   on. (The overlapping red and yellow will give
   an orange colour, the yellow and blue will
   make a green colour, and the blue and red
   will make a purple shade.)

4

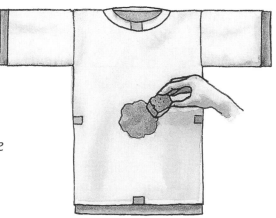

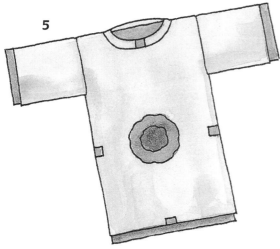

5

6   Carry on sponging circular bands of colour onto the T-shirt, using each colour in turn. Keep the same sponge for each separate colour. Make the design as big or as small as you like. You may wish to paint one large rainbow circle in the centre of the T-shirt and two smaller ones on each sleeve. Or try sponging several small rainbow circles all over the T-shirt.

7   Allow the paint to dry, leaving the card inside. Paint the back of the T-shirt in the same way, using a clean piece of card to protect the fabric.

8   Most fabric paints need to be 'fixed' (this makes the colour permanent and washable), but check the manufacturer's instructions. To fix most brands of fabric paint: cover the painted area with a clean cotton cloth and iron for 1–2 minutes on the hottest setting. Ask an adult to help you do this. For best results wash the garment again before you wear it.

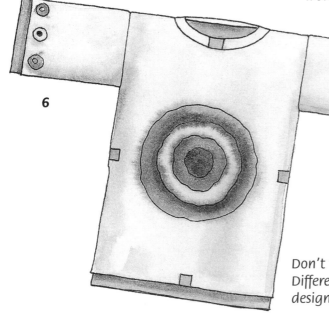

6

Don't worry if the paint doesn't go on evenly. Differences in shade and texture will make the design look more attractive.

7. WANDERING IN THE DESERT

Many years later Jacob's descendants, the Israelites, were living miserably as slaves in Egypt. God sent a man called Moses to free them from slavery and lead them back to Canaan, the Promised Land.

The journey from Egypt was a long and difficult one – a journey that was to take them 40 years. The land they travelled through was an empty wilderness, a dry and dusty desert.

'God himself will lead us home,' Moses told the people of Israel. And so God did. By day he went before them as a pillar of cloud to show them the way. At night God led the Israelites by a pillar of fire, so they could travel both day and night.

When the pillar of cloud or fire moved, so the people moved. But if it remained in one place, the people stayed, pitching their tents and setting up camps.

Exodus 13

Desert Scene Theatre

This desert scene theatre is ideal for acting out your favourite Bible stories – including many featured in this book. If you wish, you can change the scenery simply by painting different background scenes on separate pieces of card (cut to the same size as your box) and sliding them into place. Try painting an underwater theme for the stories of Noah and Jonah, or a city wall for the story of Rahab and the spies.

YOU WILL NEED:

a large cardboard box

cardboard scraps

scissors and a craft knife

a pencil, paints and brushes, felt-tip pens

masking tape

a tape measure

PVA glue and brush

material (for the theatre curtains)

a needle and thread, and a large darning needle

narrow elastic (about 4 times as long as the width of your box)

'invisible' nylon thread

small paper clips

1 Cut one long flap and both small side flaps off the top of the cardboard box. (Keep the side flaps to make the theatre wings.) Stand the box on its side so that the remaining flap is at the top. Draw a fancy shape on the flap for the theatre top. Cut out around it.

2 To keep the theatre top upright, cut a narrow strip from a scrap of cardboard. Tape one end of the strip to the back of the theatre top and the other end to the top of the box.

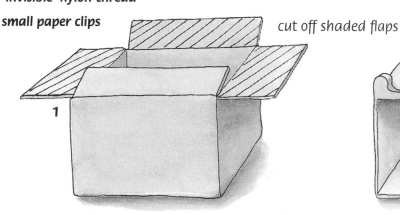

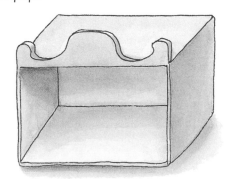

cut off shaded flaps

3   You will need to cut a hole in the top of the box. First draw a line widthways across the centre of the box. Then, leaving a border of 2.5cm (1in) around the back and sides, draw an inner panel on the back half of the box. Ask an adult to cut out the panel with a craft knife.

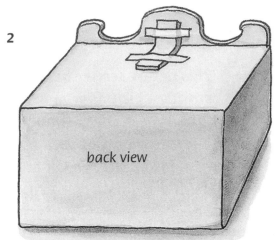

2

back view

4   Paint the outside of the theatre in bright colours. Paint the inside with a desert scene of palm trees, sand, rocky hills, blue sky and sun. If your box is uneven at the back, paint your scenery onto some card cut to fit the inside of the box. Slide it in when dry.

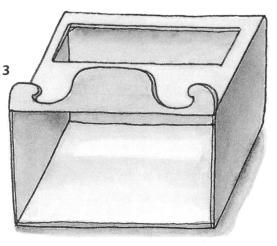

3

5   Make 2 side wings for the theatre, using the box's side flaps kept from Step 1. Cut each wing to the width you wish. Draw a palm tree or tent on each one, painting the background to match the rest of the scenery. Glue the wings on either side of the stage, positioning them just in front of the cut-out panel.

4

5

position wing just in front of cut out panel on top of box

6 To make the curtains, measure the width and depth of the theatre front. Add 10cm (4in) to the width measurement and 5cm (2in) to the depth, to allow for hems. Cut out a piece of material to this size, then fold it in half widthways. Cut down the centre fold, so that you have 2 curtains of equal size. Hem the sides, top and bottom of each curtain, making the top hem big enough to thread the elastic through.

6

elastic threads through loop at top

back of curtain

7

back   front

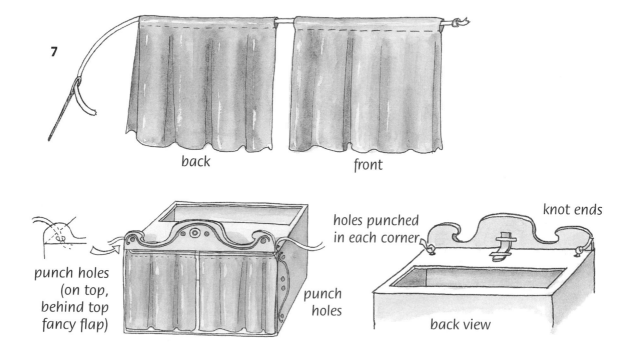

punch holes (on top, behind top fancy flap)

punch holes

holes punched in each corner

knot ends

back view

8

Pull elastic tight. Knot ends.

back

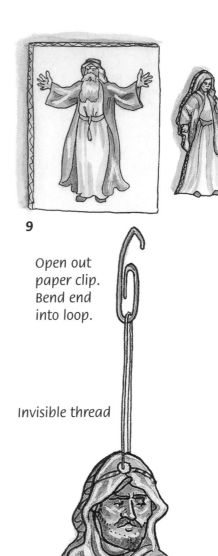

9

Open out paper clip. Bend end into loop.

Invisible thread

cardboard figure

7   Cut the elastic into 3 equal lengths. Thread one length onto a large darning needle and knot the end. Now punch the needle down through the top left-hand corner of the theatre box (just behind the theatre top). Pull the elastic through the hole until it is secured by the knot. Thread the curtains onto the elastic. Bring the curtains and elastic across the front of the theatre, then punch the needle up through the top right-hand corner. Tie a knot in the end, pulling the elastic taut. You should be able to open and close your curtains easily.

8   Using the same method as above, stretch 2 evenly spaced lines of elastic across the cut-out panel on the theatre. Your Bible figures will hang from these elastic lines.

9   Draw pictures of your favourite Bible characters onto scraps of cardboard. Cut the figures out, then paint on both sides, or colour in with felt-tip pens.

10 Punch a needle, threaded with 'invisible' nylon thread, through the top of each cardboard figure. Bend one end of a paper clip into a loop and tie the thread to the clip (you will need to adjust the length so the figures will stand upright on the theatre floor). The figures can then easily be hung and moved along the elastic lines at the back of the box, like puppets. You can hide the figures behind the wings when you do not want them to be seen during your theatre show.

Slide figures along elastic (or hide behind wings when off stage)

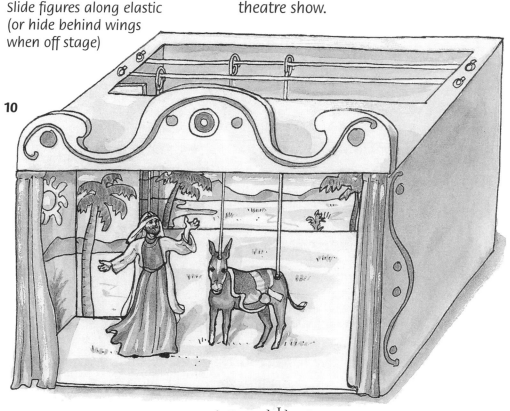

Tips and Ideas

☀ Add curtain ties. Punch a hole on either side of the theatre box and thread through some narrow ribbon.
☀ To make sparkly curtains, sew sequins or tiny gold stars to your curtains.

8. MOSES RECEIVES THE LAW FROM GOD

Three months after leaving Egypt, the Israelites arrived at the foot of Mount Sinai. Moses climbed up the mountain to talk with God.

'In three days I will speak to the people,' God told him. 'If they obey my laws I will make them my holy nation.'

On the third day there was loud thunder and lightning, and the mountain shook and billowed with smoke and fire.

God called Moses up to him and said, 'I am the Lord your God who brought you out of Egypt:

1   You shall have no other God but me.
2   Do not make any picture or statue to worship.
3   Do not use my name wrongly or without respect.
4   Keep the Sabbath day holy.
5   Respect your mother and father.
6   Do not kill.
7   Keep faithful to your husband or wife.
8   Do not steal.
9   Do not lie.
10 Do not envy another person's possessions.'

God wrote the Ten Commandments on tablets of stone. He gave Moses many other laws, and Moses wrote them all down on holy scrolls.

Exodus 19–20

Scrolls

You can make these scrolls into unusual and novel birthday or congratulations cards for your friends and family. Or why not turn one into a 'Do Not Disturb!' sign to hang on your bedroom door?

YOU WILL NEED:

a bamboo cane

sandpaper

a sheet of A3 paper

scissors

a used, damp teabag

strong glue (such as UHU)

a 51cm (20in) length of ribbon

felt-tip pens

1   Ask an adult to cut off two 36cm (14in) lengths from the cane, and smooth the rough edges with sandpaper.

1

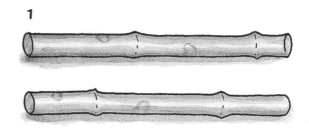

2   If you want to make the scroll look old, cut down the long sides of the paper to give a worn, jagged edge. Then rub a used, squeezed-out teabag over both sides of the paper to give a yellowed finish. Leave to dry.

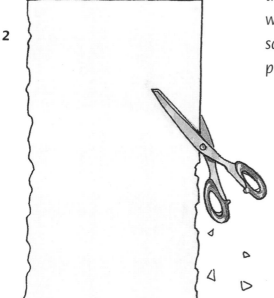

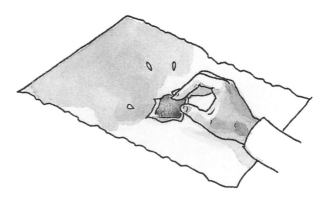

3 Dab glue onto one of the cane lengths and along one short edge of the paper. Fold the paper around the cane and stick down firmly. Repeat with the second cane at the opposite end of the paper. Leave to dry.

4 Glue the centre point of the ribbon to the back of the scroll, in the middle of the top cane. Leave to dry.

5 Write or draw a message on the front of the scroll, then roll it up loosely from the bottom and tie with the ribbon. The ribbon can also be used to hang the scroll up.

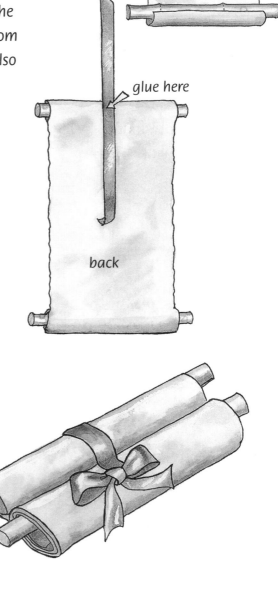

3

glue down

front

glue here

back

5

Happy Birthday Dad

9. SPIES ON A MISSION

God said to Moses, 'Send men ahead to spy out Canaan, the land I am giving to your people.'

So Moses sent out leaders from each of the 12 tribes of Israel. They explored the country and when they returned 40 days later, the people gathered round them, eager for news.

'Canaan is a rich country, flowing with milk and honey!' the spies reported back. 'But the people living there are very strong. Their cities are large and well protected. We shall never be able to overcome them.'

Then one of the spies, a man called Caleb, spoke directly to Moses. 'Let us advance on Canaan at once,' he advised. 'With God's help, we can easily conquer it.'

Still the others were afraid. 'The Canaanites are far too powerful for us – they look like giants!' they told the people. 'Compared to them we felt like tiny grasshoppers!'

Numbers 13

Secret Codes and Messages

Spies need to keep information hidden from the enemy. One way of passing on a message in secret is to use a code. The person a spy sends messages to is called a contact or codebreaker. To decode the message the codebreaker must know the code being used, or have a copy of it, kept in a code book.

SYMBOL CODES

In this type of code, a sign or symbol is used in place of each letter of the alphabet (see below). You can use any symbols you like to make up your own code.

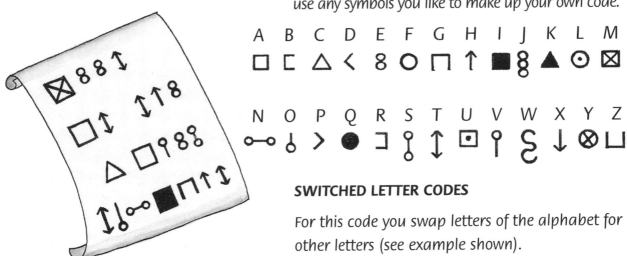

SWITCHED LETTER CODES

For this code you swap letters of the alphabet for other letters (see example shown).

starter letter
↓

A B C D E F G H I J K L M N O P Q R S T U V W X Y Z
M N O P Q R S T U V W X Y Z A B C D E F G H I J K L

↑
start 2nd alphabet here

1 Write out the alphabet along the top of a piece of paper.
2 Choose any letter, except A, for your starter letter (O in the example shown).

3 Write A under your chosen letter. Continue writing out a second alphabet directly under the first one.

4 When you get to Z in the top alphabet, go back to the beginning of your second line (underneath the top A), and continue from there.

5 To write your message in code, find the letter you want to use from the top alphabet and swap it for the letter written underneath.

6 Do not forget to let your codebreaker know which letter you began with, so that your message can be decoded. You could use the first letter of a secret password which only you and your contact know. To confuse your enemy even further, keep changing your code by using a different starter letter.

YOU WILL NEED:

lemon juice

a fine paint brush

plain white paper

INVISIBLE WRITING

One way of sending really top secret messages is to use invisible writing.

1 Squeeze a little lemon juice into a saucer.

2 Dip the brush in the juice and use it to write your message.

3 Let the paper dry completely before sending your message.

4 To make your message visible again, gently iron the paper, written side up, using an iron on a warm/medium setting. After a few moments the lemon juice will turn brown.

10. BALAAM'S TALKING DONKEY

In time the Israelites neared the border of Moab. Balek, King of Moab, was terrified at their arrival.

'There are far too many Israelites for us to defeat in battle!' he told his advisors. 'Let's send for Balaam the holy man and ask him to curse these people. Then we might win a victory over them.'

When Balek's messengers arrived, Balaam refused to go with them – at first. Already God had told him, 'You must not curse my people, they are blessed.'

But later he did agree to go and set off on his donkey. God was angry at this and sent an angel with a drawn sword to bar his way.

Balaam saw nothing, but three times his donkey swerved off the road to escape the angel's sword. Angrily, Balaam beat his animal, until it spoke to him!

'Why do you hit me?' it asked.

'Because you refuse to obey me,' Balaam replied.

Then suddenly, God opened Balaam's eyes and he too saw the angel. The angel commanded Balaam to meet with Balek as arranged. But to Balek's horror, Balaam did not curse the Israelites. Instead he showered them with many great blessings!

Numbers 22

Dinky Donkey

This toy would make a lovely present for a younger brother or sister.

YOU WILL NEED:

a broom handle

a large, plain, coloured sock

newspaper or old tights (for stuffing)

felt (for the ears)

scissors

pins, needles and thread

tape measure

paper

thick wool in a variety of colours

2 buttons (for the eyes)

1 metre (1 yard) of narrow tape or ribbon (for the bridle and reins)

2 small curtain rings

2 round bells (available from craft or pet shops)

2 metres (2½ yards) of narrow

coloured ribbon (for fastening and decorating the broom handle)

strong, clear glue

1   Stuff the foot of the sock firmly with newspaper or old tights.

2   Cut 2 donkey ear shapes out of the felt. Fold each ear in half and pin in place on the sock head. Sew the ears on, taking the stitches a little way up on the inner side of each ear to hold it upright.

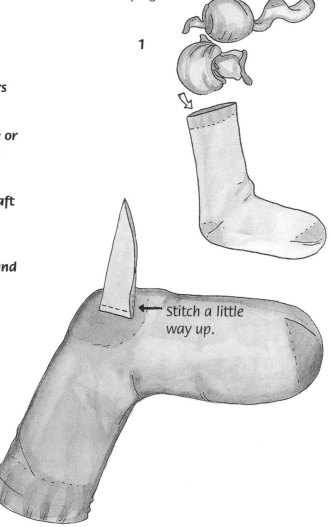

Stitch a little way up.

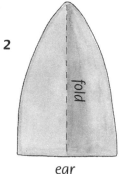

ear

3

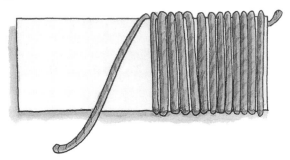

3   To make the mane, cut a piece of paper about 7.5cm (3in) wide and 20cm (8in) long. Starting at one end, begin winding wool thickly round and round the paper, until you have completely covered it.

4   Pin the wool and paper mane to the sock head. Using a needle threaded with wool, stitch down the middle of the mane to sew it to the head. Use a backstitch and take the needle through the paper. Sew tightly, catching in 3 or 4 wool loops for every stitch.

5   Cut across the wool loops on either side of the mane. Very carefully tear away the paper.

4

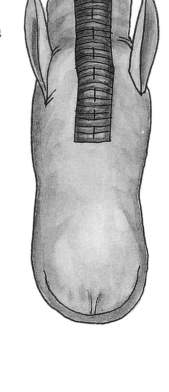

Pull paper off each side after cutting

5

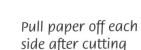

-40-

6

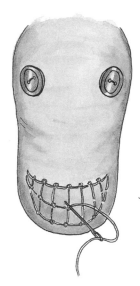

6 Sew on the buttons for eyes. Use wool to sew on an open mouth in backstitch. To sew the teeth, make the downward stitches first, then sew across the middle, looping the needle back around each tooth.

7 To make the bridle and reins, measure around the donkey's nose and add on 5cm (2in). Cut a length from the tape or ribbon you are using for the bridle to this size. Cut this length in half. Sew the 2 tape pieces onto the curtain rings to make a loop for the bridle.

7

Loop the ribbon over the curtain hooks. Sew in place (allow $^1/2/1^1/2$ cm facing)

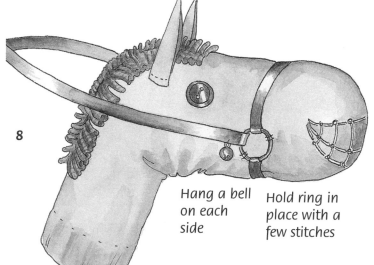

8

Hang a bell on each side

Hold ring in place with a few stitches

8 Push the bridle over the donkey's nose. Stitch the curtain rings to the sock, to keep the bridle in place. To make the reins, sew the ends of the remaining length of tape to either side of the curtain rings. Hang or sew a bell on each side of the reins, near the curtain rings.

9 Cut a 30cm (12in) length off the ribbon you are using to decorate the broom handle. Put it aside for later. Glue one end of the remaining length of ribbon to the top of the broom handle. Wind the ribbon round and round the handle (so that it looks like a candy stick), using glue to stick it down as you go. Glue the end. Leave to dry.

10 Push the broom handle into the leg of the sock. Pack stuffing around it and tie firmly with the small, leftover piece of ribbon.

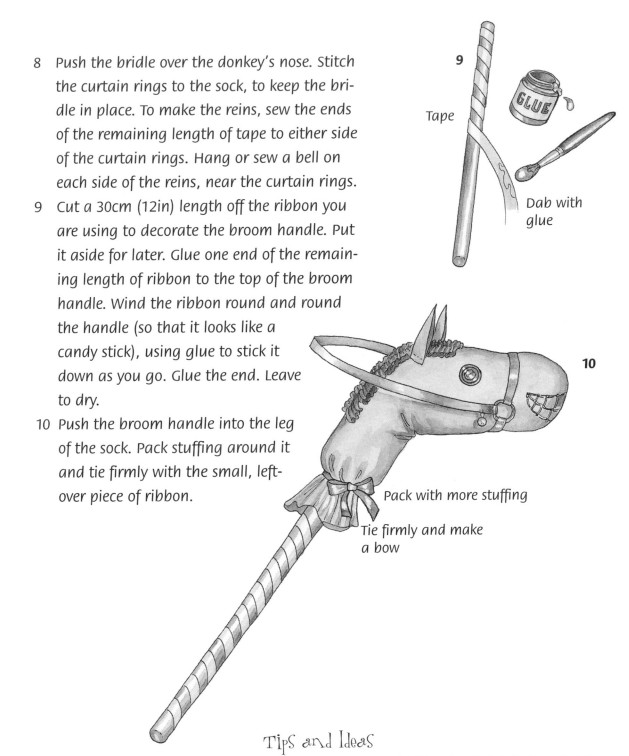

9

Tape

GLUE

Dab with glue

10

Pack with more stuffing

Tie firmly and make a bow

Tips and Ideas

☀ Why not make your bridle and reins from brightly coloured wool cords (see page 44)?

11. SAVED BY A SCARLET CORD

The Israelites had almost reached Canaan. Only the River Jordan stood between them and the Promised Land. Moses had died and Joshua was their new leader.

Joshua sent two men into Canaan to spy out the city of Jericho. There, they lodged in the house of a woman called Rahab.

The King of Jericho soon discovered that spies were in his city. 'Go and capture them!' he ordered his soldiers.

When Rahab heard the soldiers knocking at her door, she quickly hid the Israelites on the roof, under some flax, so they would not be seen.

When the danger had passed she told the spies, 'We know that God is on your side. Everyone here is terrified of you. I saved your life – will you promise to spare me and my family when you conquer Jericho?'

The men agreed. Now Rahab's house was built into the city walls. 'Hang a scarlet rope from your window,' they told her. 'Then we will know not to harm anyone inside your home.'

Afterwards, when the Israelites attacked the city, they kept their promise to Rahab. All her family were spared.

Joshua 2

Colourful Cords! Beautiful Braids!

These wool cords are great fun and really easy to make. Use them to make pretty hair ties, fancy belts or friendship bracelets. They can be as long and as colourful as you wish.

YOU WILL NEED:

wool in assorted colours

scissors

a friend (or two!)

1 Cut 3 (or more) strands of different coloured wool, $2^1/_2$ times the length you want your finished cord to be. The more strands you use, the thicker the cord will be.

2 Get a friend to help you. You hold the 3 lengths of wool at one end, while your friend holds them at the other end. Face each other and hold the wool taut between you.

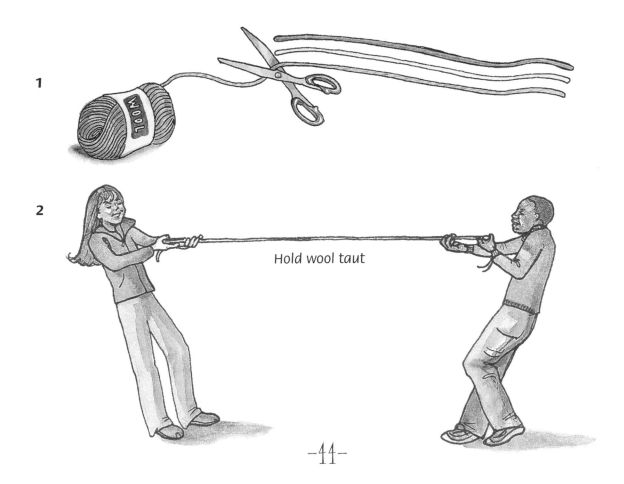

1

2

Hold wool taut

3

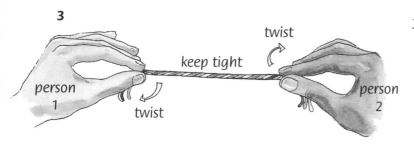

person 1   keep tight   twist   person 2

twist

4

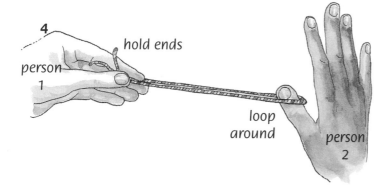

hold ends

person 1

loop around

person 2

5

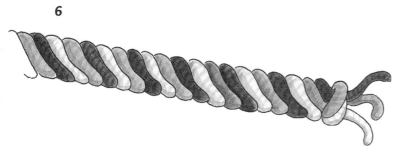

shake!

6

3 Now both of you start twisting the wool in a clockwise direction (towards the right) – that is, in opposite directions to each other. Keep twisting, holding the wool taut, until it feels springy.

4 One person should now take hold of both ends, while the other person quickly puts his or her finger in the centre of the cord to keep it straight. When making very long cords, have a third person on hand to help with this stage!

5 As the person holding the wool in the centre lets go, the person holding the ends must shake the wool sharply. It will then form itself into a colourful, twisted cord.

6 If necessary, smooth the cord with your hands. Knot both ends, trim them and fluff out to make pretty tassels.

12. SAMSON THE SUPER-STRONG

Samson was born at a time when the Israelites were being defeated by their enemies, the Philistines.

He was a rough, tough man with amazing strength – and a secret! Born a Nazirite dedicated to God, he knew he must never cut his hair, or else his strength would disappear.

The Philistines hated Samson. One day he killed a thousand of their soldiers using the jawbone of a donkey. They determined to find out the secret behind his strength.

'Samson is in love with Delilah, a Philistine girl,' they plotted. 'We'll pay her to help us.'

Delilah agreed. All day, every day, she nagged Samson, saying, 'Tell me your secret.' And one day, he did.

While Samson slept, Delilah had his head shaved. The Philistines came for him, but Samson was powerless to fight back. He was blinded and thrown into prison – but then his hair began to grow back.

One day the Philistines brought him into their temple, to mock him.

'Oh Lord,' Samson prayed, 'give me enough strength to take revenge on my enemies.' Pushing hard against the temple pillars with all his might, he brought the building crashing down. Everyone died.

Judges 13–16

Hairy Samson

YOU WILL NEED:

a 10p piece

a clean, empty plastic yoghurt pot (with the label removed)

a pencil

scissors

a clean and empty hardboiled egg shell (carefully broken at the widest end)

scraps of card

clear glue

acrylic or poster paints and brushes

cotton wool

a packet of cress seeds

water

1   Place the 10p piece on the base of the yoghurt pot and draw around it with a pencil. Cut out the drawn circle.

1

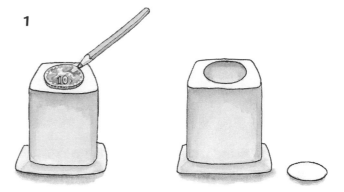

2   Place the empty egg shell into the hole, open end up, to check that it holds well (the shell will be Samson's head). Cut the hole a little larger if needed. Remove the egg shell.

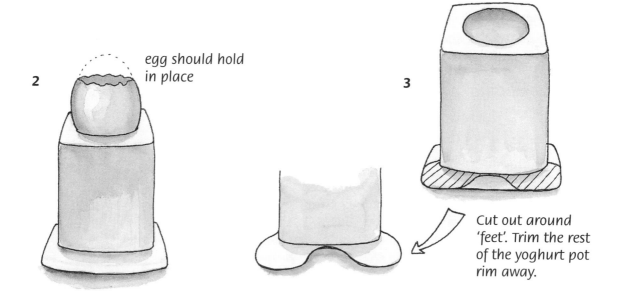

2 egg should hold in place

3

Cut out around 'feet'. Trim the rest of the yoghurt pot rim away.

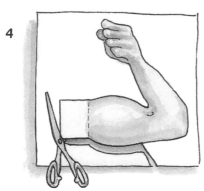

4

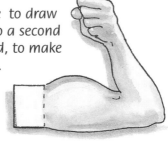

Cut out. Use to draw around onto a second piece of card, to make second arm.

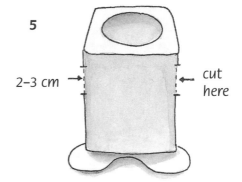

5

2–3 cm →   ← cut here

3 With a pencil, draw 2 foot shapes on opposite corners of one side of the yoghurt pot rim. Cut out around your pencil marks, then trim off the rest of the rim, cutting all the way round.

4 Draw a hand and arm shape onto card. Make the arm look muscled. Allow an extra 1–2cm ($^{1}/_{2}$ – $^{3}/_{4}$in) tab at the top of the arm for slotting into the yoghurt pot. Cut the arm out, then draw around the shape onto another piece of card, and cut that out to make a second arm.

5 Use scissors to cut 2 slits on either side of the yoghurt pot, for the arms to slot into. Each slit should be 2–3cm (1in) long.

6 Slot the tab ends of each arm into the cut slits.

7 Dab glue around the edges of the hole on the top of the pot. Stick on the egg shell head. Allow the glue to dry.

6

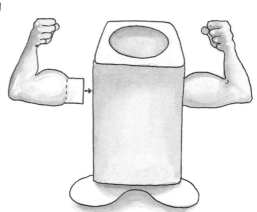

7

GLUE

8

8   Paint the model all over, allowing each colour to dry before painting on another. Use a flesh colour for the face, arms and chest, then paint a funny costume onto the body, and finally add the eyes, nose and mouth to the face.

9   When the model is completely dry, place a small wad of cotton wool in the bottom of the egg shell. Sprinkle a thin layer of cress seeds on top, then pour in enough water to fully moisten the cotton wool. (Check the cress packet instructions.)

10   Place in a light, warm spot. Check each day that the cotton wool is still damp. In a few days the seeds will begin to sprout, and Samson will grow hair!

9

10

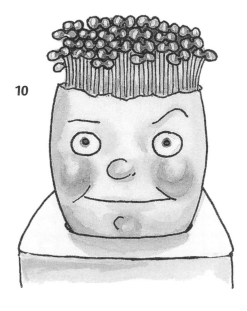

13. DAVID THE SHEPHERD BOY

David was a young shepherd boy who became Israel's greatest ever King.

He spent his youth in the fields, looking after his father's sheep. David sang and played the harp beautifully. He wrote many psalms in praise and worship of God. In Psalm 23, David compares God to a good shepherd who cares for his own people in the same way that a shepherd watches over his sheep.

The Lord is my shepherd,
  I shall not want.
He makes me lie down in
  green pastures.
He leads me beside still waters;
  he restores my soul.
He leads me in paths of righteousness,
  for his name's sake.

Samuel 16; Psalm 23:1–3

Snazzy Sheep Coat Hooks

YOU WILL NEED:

thin cardboard

pencil and compass

scissors

clear, strong glue

acrylic paints and brushes

scraps of black, white and pink felt

a medium-sized white cup hook

Blu-Tack

Remember to ask permission before screwing the hook into your wall.

1 Use a pencil and compass to draw a circle 20cm (7¹/₂in) in diameter onto a piece of thin cardboard.

2 Draw a rough scallop edge all the way round the outside edge of the circle, to make it look woolly. Cut the whole shape out.

3 Place the shape onto another piece of card. Draw around it with a pencil and cut the second shape out.

4 Draw a large, egg-shaped head (with the widest end at the top), in the middle of the first piece of card. Position the head slightly above the centre. Cut it out. (To cut the head out easily, use scissors to make a hole in the centre. Then make several slits fanning out from the hole to the edge of your pencil marks, before finally cutting out around them.)

1

2

3

cut out
2nd shape

1st shape

4

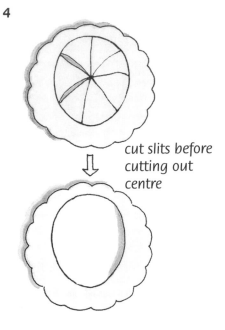

cut slits before
cutting out
centre

5   Cut out 2 large ear shapes from cardboard,
    allowing 2cm (³/₄in) extra at the bottom for
    an overlap.

6   Place the head shape with the cut-out face
    on top of the other head shape. Slide the
    ears into place between the 2 cardboard lay-
    ers, making sure the ends do not poke out
    onto the inner face. When you are happy
    with the position of the ears, remove the top
    head and glue the ears to the base head.

7   Now glue the top head to the base head,
    sandwiching the ears in between, and
    matching up the scalloped edges. Press
    together firmly until the glue is dry.

8   Paint the sheep's woolly outer rim with white
    acrylic paint. Then paint the inner face and
    ears in black. Wash your brushes between
    colours.

5

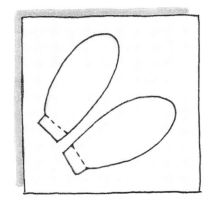

6

7

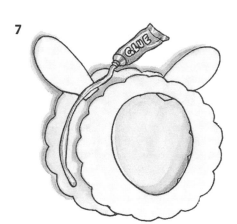

8

9

9 Cut out 2 large oval eyes from white felt, and 2 small round eyes from black felt. Glue the black eyes near the bottom of the white eyes, then glue both eyes quite close together onto the sheep's face. Cut out a pink felt tongue. Glue the top only, so that the tongue can flap, and press into position at the bottom of the face.

glue top of tongue only

10 Push the cup hook through the sheep's face, where the nose would be. Ask an adult to help you screw the hook to your wall or door. Before you do this, stick some Blu-Tack to the back of the sheep to help hold it upright once the hook is screwed in.

10

Tips and Ideas

☀ Poster paints look just as good as acrylic paints, but you will need to varnish your paint work to prevent any colour from rubbing onto clothes hung on the hook.

14. THE QUEEN OF SHEBA BRINGS GIFTS TO SOLOMON

King Solomon of Israel was known throughout the land for his great wisdom and wealth. News travels far, and his fame soon reached the ears of the Queen of Sheba, far away in Arabia.

'I must visit Solomon myself, and discover if these wise judgements he is famous for are true,' she decided.

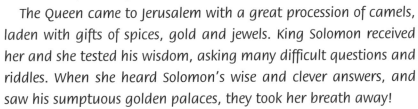

The Queen came to Jerusalem with a great procession of camels, laden with gifts of spices, gold and jewels. King Solomon received her and she tested his wisdom, asking many difficult questions and riddles. When she heard Solomon's wise and clever answers, and saw his sumptuous golden palaces, they took her breath away!

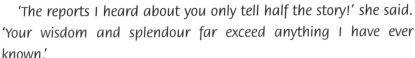

'The reports I heard about you only tell half the story!' she said. 'Your wisdom and splendour far exceed anything I have ever known.'

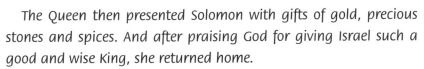

The Queen then presented Solomon with gifts of gold, precious stones and spices. And after praising God for giving Israel such a good and wise King, she returned home.

Kings 10

Great Gift Boxes

YOU WILL NEED:

thin, coloured card

a pencil and ruler

scissors

strong, clear glue (such as UHU)

decorative materials (see suggestions below)

Fill these little boxes with sweets or tiny gifts to make someone an extra special present. The instructions below will make a 6cm (2½in) square box.

1. First take a look at diagram 1 below. Using a ruler and pencil, copy out the same shape onto a piece of card, making each square 6cm x 6cm (2½in x 2½in). Draw on 1.5cm (½in) flaps where shown in the picture. Cut out the whole shape.

2. Fold up the card to make a box shape, following diagram 2. Glue the 4 side flaps inside the box to hold it together. Do not glue the top flap – that tucks in and out, to open and close the box.

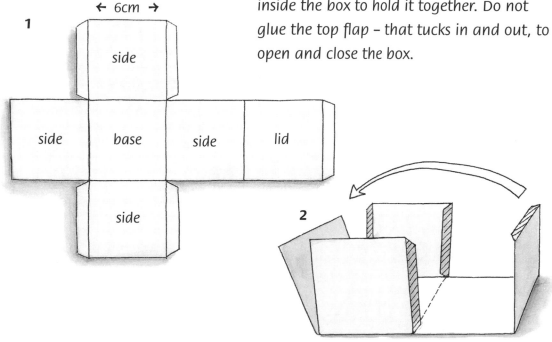

1

← 6cm →

side

side   base   side   lid

side

2

  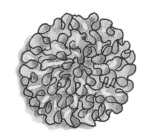

DECORATING YOUR BOX

Here are a few ideas to get you going!

1 Cut out 3 small circles from pretty coloured tissue paper. Lay them on top of each other and staple them together in the centre. Starting at the top, crinkle each layer in your hand to form a flower. Cut out three leaves from green tissue paper. Glue these to the top of your box, then glue the tissue paper flower on top.

2 Try sticking small, pretty shells onto your box. Decorate the spaces between the shells with drawings of tiny fish or starfish.

3 Cut out squares of lace and stick them to the sides of the box. Top with a ribbon bow. This looks great if you make your box with a dark-coloured card.

15. DANIEL AND THE DANGEROUS LIONS

Daniel was a good and trustworthy man. He loved God and prayed to him daily. King Darius of Persia greatly admired Daniel, and appointed him ruler over his kingdom. However, this made his other officials jealous.

'We must get rid of Daniel,' they decided, and hurried to the King with a plan.

'We have drawn up a new law,' they told Darius. 'For the next 30 days no one may pray to anyone but you. Whoever disobeys must be thrown to the lions!'

The King agreed, but although Daniel heard of the law he did not stop praying to God. Triumphantly the officials returned to the King.

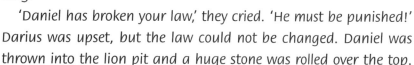

'Daniel has broken your law,' they cried. 'He must be punished!' Darius was upset, but the law could not be changed. Daniel was thrown into the lion pit and a huge stone was rolled over the top.

Early next morning, the King raced to the pit. 'Daniel!' he called out. 'Has your God been able to save you?'

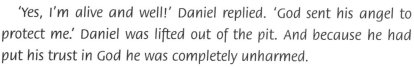

'Yes, I'm alive and well!' Daniel replied. 'God sent his angel to protect me.' Daniel was lifted out of the pit. And because he had put his trust in God he was completely unharmed.

Daniel 6

Lion Photograph Frame

YOU WILL NEED:

a photograph (a horizontal, rectangular picture is best)

a sheet of plain paper

a pencil and ruler

scissors and a craft knife

strong card

thick poster paints and brushes

clear varnish and brush

strong glue

masking tape

1 Place the photograph in the middle of a sheet of paper and draw around it. Then draw a second line 0.5cm (¹/₄in) inside the first. This will be the area of your photograph when the frame is finished.

2 Draw a lion-shaped frame around the inner line. It does not matter if part of the lion (e.g. the mane or tail) overlaps a little into the area where your photograph will be.

3 When you are happy with your drawing, cut it out around the outside. Then cut out the inner shape, remembering not to cut off any overlapping mane or tail.

1

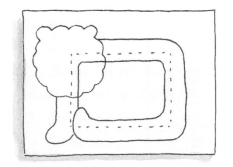

2

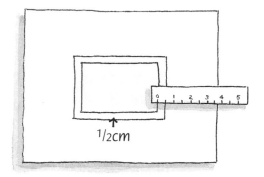

¹/₂cm

3

cut out

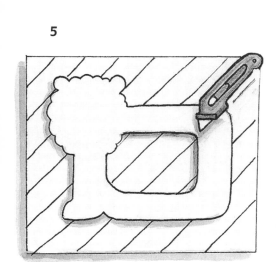

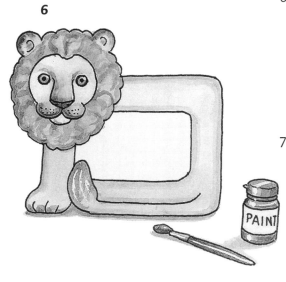

4   To make the base of the frame: place the paper lion shape onto a piece of card. Draw around the outside with a pencil. Cut it out.

5   To make the front of the frame: place the paper lion shape onto another piece of card. Draw around the outside and then around the inner hole. Cut out around the outside, and then ask an adult to help you cut out the inner shape with a craft knife.

6   Paint the front of the frame to look like a lion. Add some features, like a bushy tail and mane, claws, eyes, nose and a mouth. Leave to dry, then brush on a coat of varnish to stop the frame from chipping. Allow that to dry.

7   Glue the photograph into position on the base of the frame. Dab more glue around the outer edges, taking care not to get glue on the photograph itself. Then stick the painted frame on top, making sure that the top and bottom shapes match up exactly. Leave to dry.

7

join
together
↓

8   To make a flap for the back of the frame, cut out a piece of card about three-quarters of the height and one-third of the width of the frame. Line up one of the short edges of the flap with the bottom edge of the frame. Tape the flap at the top with a strip of masking tape. Open the flap slightly to allow the picture to stand up.

8

back view

picture

16. JONAH AND THE GREAT WHALE

'Jonah!' God said. 'Go to Nineveh and tell the people there to change their evil ways.'

But Jonah refused to go, and jumped on a ship headed in the opposite direction, to Tarshish.

While the ship was at sea, a dreadful storm blew up. 'We're all going to drown!' the sailors cried fearfully. 'What have we done to deserve this fate?'

Jonah knew that he was the cause of their troubles. 'I've disobeyed God,' he said. 'Throw me into the sea and the storm will die down.'

When the sailors dropped Jonah overboard, the waves immediately calmed. Jonah was swallowed by a whale and for three days he lay inside its belly.

'Oh Lord,' he prayed, 'please save me!'

God heard Jonah's prayers and told the fish to cough him out safely onto the shore.

'Now will you go to Nineveh?' God asked.

Jonah went at once. 'Stop sinning!' he warned the people. 'Or in 40 days God will destroy this great city.'

The people listened to the message and were afraid. Quickly they changed their ways, and begged God to forgive them. Pleased, God was merciful and spared them.

Jonah

Big Fish Money Box

Make this fun fish money box – and watch it swallow up your money!

YOU WILL NEED:

a small balloon

a cardboard packing tube with a plastic, push-in stopper

scissors and a craft knife

masking tape

newspaper

PVA glue (diluted 1 part water to 2 parts glue) or flour paste (see recipe on page 17), and brush

small pieces of card

a pencil

a pin

thick poster paints and brushes

clear varnish

1 Blow up the balloon to the size you want the fish to be. Tie a knot in it.

2 Ask an adult to cut off 2–3cm (1in) from one end of the packing tube, using a craft knife. Take out the stopper, but do not throw it away.

3 Tape the cut end of the tube piece onto the balloon. This will make the base for the fish.

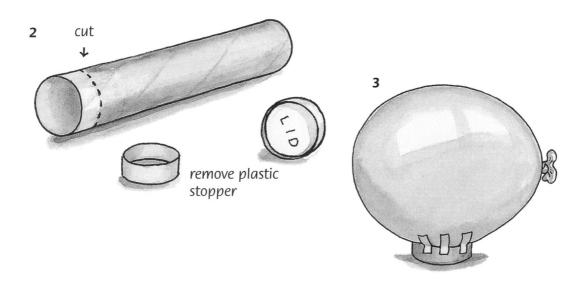

2 cut

remove plastic stopper

LID

3

4

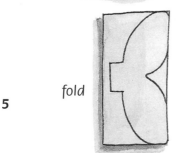

5 fold

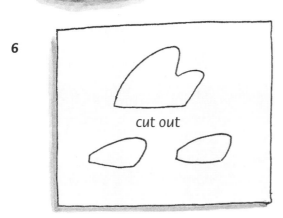

4   Tear the newspaper into small strips, about 7cm x 5cm (3in x 2in) in size. Brush the strips with paste and stick all over the balloon and the outside of the base, until both are completely covered. Do the same with more strips of paper, until you have built up 5 layers of the papier-mâchè. Leave for about 2 days to dry and harden properly.

5   Fold a piece of card in half. Draw a fish tail shape, positioning the 2 outer tips of the tail on the fold. Cut out around the tail shape, making sure that you do not cut through the fold. Fan out the tail a little and tape it in place on the fish.

6   cut out

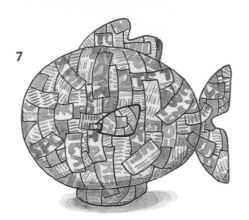

7

8

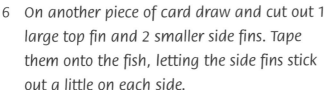

6 On another piece of card draw and cut out 1 large top fin and 2 smaller side fins. Tape them onto the fish, letting the side fins stick out a little on each side.

7 Cover the balloon, base, tail and fins with 2 more layers of papier-mâchè. Leave to dry thoroughly.

8 Pop the balloon with a pin, and pull it out through the base of the fish.

9 Cut a slit in the top of the fish, just behind the top fin. Make sure it is big enough to drop money through. Trim off any rough edges at the bottom of the base.

10 Paint the fish all over with white paint. When this has dried, paint it in bright colours. Allow to dry again, then finish off with a coat of varnish. When the varnish is dry, put the plastic stopper back in the base.

9 (arial view)

slit

cut off any rough edges

10